THE CLASSIC
FAIRY TALE COLLECTION

Jack and the Beanstalk

Retold by JOHN CECH

Illustrated by ROBERT MACKENZIE

STERLING

New York / London

JACK was always getting things just a little confused. Once, his mother sent him to town to buy a new rake and he came home with a chocolate cake. Another day she asked him to go fetch some wood, but instead he stretched and took a walk in the woods. So it shouldn't have surprised her that when she sent Jack off to sell their cow to improve their lot, he came home with a handful of beans—in an old pot.

"Beans!" she cried. "How could you sell our cow for beans?!"

"But the man said they were magic beans," Jack replied.

"Look, they're really beautiful."

It wouldn't have been so bad if Jack and his mother had another cow, but they were very poor, with nothing to eat and not even a cup of milk to drink.

"How are we to live on a handful of beans?" Jack's mother asked. She was so angry that she threw the beans and the pot out the window.

That night it rained. When Jack and his mother awoke the next morning, they discovered that an enormous beanstalk had sprung up overnight, right where the beans had landed, and wound its way up into the clouds.

"I think I'll see where this beanstalk leads," said Jack. His mother tried to stop him, but Jack had already scampered out of her reach up the stalk. "Maybe I'll find more beans higher up. Then we could make some bean soup."

Jack climbed and climbed. In fact, he climbed so high that he went right through the clouds! At the top of the beanstalk, he found a country like none he had ever seen before. Everything was much, much bigger—the grass came up to his knees, and the butterflies were as big as birds.

Nearby, he saw a large stone house—a castle, actually. Soon Jack found himself knocking on a huge, heavy door. It creaked open and a normal-size woman looked suspiciously through the crack at him.

"I'm lost," Jack said.

"And you'd better stay that way," the woman replied. "My husband will be coming home soon. He's a giant, and he doesn't like visitors."

"If only I could have a little something to eat," Jack pleaded, "and then I'll be on my way."

"Come in, then," she said. "But only for a few minutes."

As Jack sat eating in the kitchen, he told the woman about how he had sold the family's only cow for some beans and how his mother had thrown them out the window. Suddenly the house began to shake and the front door slammed.

"Quick, get under the table," the woman whispered to Jack as she lifted the tablecloth and showed him a place where he could hide.

"What's for dinner?" the giant asked.

"Your favorite meal," his wife replied. "Giant pie with
a dozen crusty baguettes. And for dessert . . ."

But before she could finish, the giant sniffed the air
and bellowed:

Fee Fi Fo Fum,
I smell a visitor, yum, yum, yum.
Fish or fowl, cold or hot,
We'll cook him up inside my pot.

You see, the giant only liked company that
he could serve up for dinner.

"I'm very sorry, my dear," his wife said, "but you must be imagining things. There's no one here except you, me, and the goose."

But the giant still sensed a guest somewhere in the house. He looked everywhere—except under the table, where Jack was holding his breath.

When the giant was done searching his house, he sat down and quickly devoured his supper. Then he called for his goose, and she waddled over from her nest in the next room. He picked her up, placed her on the table, and commanded her, "Lay, lay, lay! Lay, lay, lay!"

And she did—egg after egg after egg of pure gold! The goose kept laying eggs until the giant grew tired of the game. His eyes began to droop, and he fell asleep right there at the table.

When the giant began to snore, his wife reached under the table and pulled Jack out by the collar of his shirt.

"Quick!" she whispered. "Leave before he wakes up!" Seeing the golden eggs and the goose, and thinking faster than he had ever thought before, Jack snatched the goose from the table, tucked her under his arm, and dashed out the door before the giant's wife could stop him. With the goose honking the whole way, Jack raced over to the beanstalk and climbed down.

At home, Jack's mother sat weeping for the son she thought had been lost forever. Suddenly Jack appeared in the kitchen. He showed her the goose and told her about the golden eggs. When the goose actually laid one of those eggs, Jack's mother began to cry even more, this time out of pure joy.

With the help of the goose and her golden eggs, Jack and his mother were soon able to fix up their farm and buy new cows. Life was very good. But then one day—no one knows why—the goose just flew away.

Jack decided to go up the beanstalk once more to try to find the goose. His mother tearfully pleaded with him not to go, but Jack was determined and told her not to worry.

Again Jack found himself knocking on the giant's door, and again the giant's wife opened the huge door just enough to look out.

"How could you come back after what you've done?" she asked him.
"Do you know what a story I had to make up to stop my husband from
ransacking all of creation for you and his precious goose? I told him the
goose just flapped her wings and flew out the window, but I don't think
he believes me even now."

Suddenly the ground began to tremble.

"Quick, come inside! You've got to hide before he gets here. If he
finds you, he'll throw us both into his pot!" With that, she tugged Jack
into the house just as the giant was rounding the corner. This time she
hid Jack in the oven.

"What's for dinner?" the giant asked.

"Another favorite," his wife replied. "I've fried a hundred smelts with truffle sauce for you, and for dessert..."

But before she could finish, the giant sniffed the air and bellowed, just like he had done the last time:

Fee Fi Fo Fum,
I smell a visitor, yum, yum, yum.
Fish or fowl, cold or hot,
We'll cook him up inside my pot.

This time the giant checked under the table first. Then he looked in all the closets and pantries and even under the sofas. But he didn't check the oven because he thought no one could possibly be hiding in there.

Finally the giant settled into his chair and gobbled up his supper, right down to the last smelt. "Wife," he called out, "bring me my sack."

The giant's wife went to a chest in a corner of the kitchen and returned with a small, well-worn leather sack. She placed it on the table in front of him. The giant untied the strings and opened the sack.

"Roll out, roll out, roll out!" he sang. "Roll out, roll out, roll out!"

A gold coin tumbled out of the sack, then another, and another. Soon the table was filled with golden coins. The giant spent an hour counting them all into tall stacks.

Then his eyelids got heavy from so much counting, and he fell asleep.

"Quick!" the woman whispered between snores that shook the table. "And don't touch that sack," she added.

As the giant's wife went to unlock the door, Jack snatched the sack and hid it behind his back. He tiptoed out the door before she could discover that he had tricked her again, and in less time than it takes to say the days of the week, he was out the door of the castle and climbing down the beanstalk.

Jack's mother was beside herself with joy to have him home safe again. The sack didn't look like much, but the more Jack said, "Roll out," the more impressed his mother became with his latest treasure.

Soon Jack and his mother had more gold coins than they knew what to do with. They could hardly believe their good fortune. Then one day—no one knows how—the sack disappeared.

One morning soon after, Jack's mother found him in the garden looking at the beanstalk. She knew he was going to climb back up it again.

"We have everything we could ever need," she told him.

"Just one more trip," Jack said.

"But what if you don't come back this time?" his mother pleaded.

"Don't worry," Jack comforted her. "I will be back."

And up the beanstalk he went. And again he knocked at the giant's door. And again the giant's wife answered.

"I didn't think you of all people would ever show up on this doorstep again. Do you know how furious my husband was when he discovered his sack had been stolen?"

"It's the way of the world," said Jack. "In fact, someone just took it from me."

Then Jack convinced the giant's wife to invite him in for a slice of the strudel he could smell cooling in the kitchen.

But before he could take his first bite, the giant came thundering home.

"Quick!" said the giant's wife. She hid Jack in a big wooden tub that she used for washing laundry and threw some bedsheets over him.

"What's for dinner?" the giant asked as he entered the room.

"Your all-time favorite," his wife replied. "Ten gallons of savory boar stew, with rosemary and squash blossoms, and a peck of parsnips on the side. And for dessert . . ."

But before she could mention the strudel, the giant sniffed the air and bellowed:

Fee Fi Fo Fum,
I smell a visitor, yum, yum, yum.
Fish or fowl, cold or hot,
We'll cook him up inside my pot.

This time the giant checked under the table and in the oven. Then he looked in the attic and the cellar and behind the curtains. But he didn't search the laundry tub, because he thought no one could possibly be hiding in there.

Finally he settled into his chair and gobbled up his supper—right down to the last morsel. Then he called out, "Wife, bring me my harp!"

The giant's wife went to a beautifully carved cabinet and unlocked it with a silver key that she kept in her apron pocket. From the cabinet she took a small golden harp.

"Play!" the giant commanded the harp, and play it did—the most beautiful melody that Jack had ever heard. The giant soon fell asleep to the music. When he began to snore, his wife tiptoed to the washtub, pulled the sheets off Jack, and pushed him toward the door.

"Quick!" she whispered. "He could wake up at any second."

Jack looked at the harp, and the giant's wife looked at him.

"I'll bring it with us," she said. "All I do up here is cook and clean, clean and cook. And all he does is moan and gripe. I'm going down the beanstalk with you."

And so she grabbed the harp and tucked it under her arm as she and Jack ran out the door together.

The giant woke up as the music faded away. When he sat up and saw that the harp was gone, he knew he had been tricked again. He charged after the sound of the music until he reached the place where the beanstalk was poking through the clouds. He almost caught Jack by the sleeve of his jacket, but Jack slipped out of his fingers and disappeared down the beanstalk. The giant was ready to climb down, too. He could hear the harp playing faintly below him. But he was frozen to the spot. You see, the giant was not afraid of many things, but he was afraid of heights. So he did what giants do. He bellowed and bellowed and bellowed. And he shook all the beans off the beanstalk. He almost shook off his wife and Jack as well, but they hung on for dear life.

When they had safely reached the ground, Jack and his neighbors cut down the beanstalk, chopped it into little pieces, and fed the pieces to their cows.

Jack's mother and the giant's wife became the best of friends. In the evenings they listened to the music of the harp as it filled their valley. To this day, people hear booming up in the clouds. They say it's the giant, still upset about all the things Jack brought down the beanstalk and about the dry crackers that he's been eating ever since his wife left.

As for Jack, well, he kept a few of the beans that fell off the beanstalk, but he never planted them. Where the beans are now, no one seems to know. Maybe you've seen them. Perhaps that's what's in the dusty jar way, way, way in the back of your kitchen cupboard.

A Note on the Story

The first story about Jack and his marvelous beanstalk appeared in England in 1734 as part of a larger collection of stories. The tale was originally titled "Jack Spriggins and the Enchanted Bean." By 1807, Jack's story had become its own book—*The History of Mother Twaddle, and the Marvellous Atchievements of Her Son Jack*—and by the late 1800s, Jack was a well-established citizen of British folklore.

Another English fairy tale features a girl in Jack's role. Her name is "Molly Whuppie," and she, too, outsmarts a giant with a strong sense of smell in order to save her little sisters and herself. Jack also traveled to America, where he became one of the favorite characters in a group of tales from the Appalachian Mountains. In one of these stories, "Jack and the Bean Tree," Jack tricks the giant just as he did when he first appeared in England. In the American version, the treasures that Jack takes down the bean stalk often include a fine hunting rifle and a magic tablecloth, as well as a hen that lays golden eggs.

In one regard, Jack is a trickster who repeatedly fools the giant and steals his most precious possessions. Yet Jack also represents every young person who, in the course of growing up, makes mistakes, braves seemingly gigantic forces, and then quickly seizes the opportunities that present themselves in life. Like the Jack tales, there are numerous stories from around the world about heroes or heroines confronting giants, ogres, and other powerful creatures (like dragons) and winning treasures possessed by them. One of the oldest known tricksters is from Homer's *The Odyssey*. In this story, the hero Odysseus fools the giant Cyclops in order to rescue himself and his traveling companions from certain death.

Ancient myths, legends, and stories also tell about ascents into the clouds. In the Bible, Jacob dreams of a ladder reaching into the sky that the angels use to move between heaven and earth. And in ancient India, Buddha is said to have sat under the Bodhi Tree, which grew to spectacular heights, in order to reach spiritual enlightenment. Norse mythology celebrates a giant ash tree called Yggdrasill, known as "the World Tree." Its uppermost branches reached into and, in fact, supported the heavens, while its roots provided mankind with the source of all wisdom. It was believed that a golden rooster lived at the top of the tree and warned the gods of attacks by the giants.

—J. C.